The Pumpkin Goblin

Makes Friends

Published by Emerald Book Company

For ordering information or special discounts for bulk purchases, please contact Emerald Book Company at: 4425 South Mo Pac Expwy., Suite 600, Austin, TX 78735, (512) 891-6100.

Design and composition by Greenleaf Book Group LLC

Publisher's Cataloging-In-Publication Data
(Prepared by The Donohue Group, Inc.)

Taylor, Aaron (Aaron L.), 1967-
  The Pumpkin Goblin makes friends / written by Aaron Taylor ; illustrated by Gary Whitley. -- 1st ed.

    p. : ill. ;   cm.

    Summary: Every year the Pumpkin Goblin terrorizes the town's children on Halloween night, but when he meets a lonely kid named Fred, the Goblin recognizes himself in the boy and has a change of heart.
    Interest age level : 003-008.
    ISBN: 978-1-934572-00-9

1. Goblins--Juvenile fiction. 2. Halloween--Juvenile fiction. 3. Friendship--Juvenile fiction. 4. Goblins--Fiction. 5. Halloween--Fiction. 6. Friendship--Fiction. I. Whitley, Gary. II. Title.

PZ7.T39567 Pum 2008
[Fic]   2008924150

Printed in China on acid-free paper

11 10 09 08   10 9 8 7 6 5 4 3 2 1

First Edition

The Pumpkin Goblin

Makes Friends

WRITTEN BY Aaron Taylor

ILLUSTRATED BY Gary Whitley

EMERALD
BOOK CO.
A Division of Greenleaf Book Group LLC

One night in the slime and grime of a bog,
A crow dropped a pumpkin seed near a dead log.

The lightning struck down, and there by the tree
Grew a Pumpkin Goblin, born to scare you and me!

His head was a pumpkin, legs and arms made of vine.
He was quite sturdy for not having a spine.

He put on some clothes found inside an old truck,
Then set off to dig worm stew from the muck.

His Green Muck Worm Stew was the best thing to eat,

When he ate from a shoe it smelled much like feet.

While he ate, he made plans for Halloween night,

To scamper and screech and give children a fright.

When Halloween came he chased all the kids.
He screeched and growled and hollered and hid.

He hid in the dark and when kids walked by,
He jumped from the spot and made everyone cry.

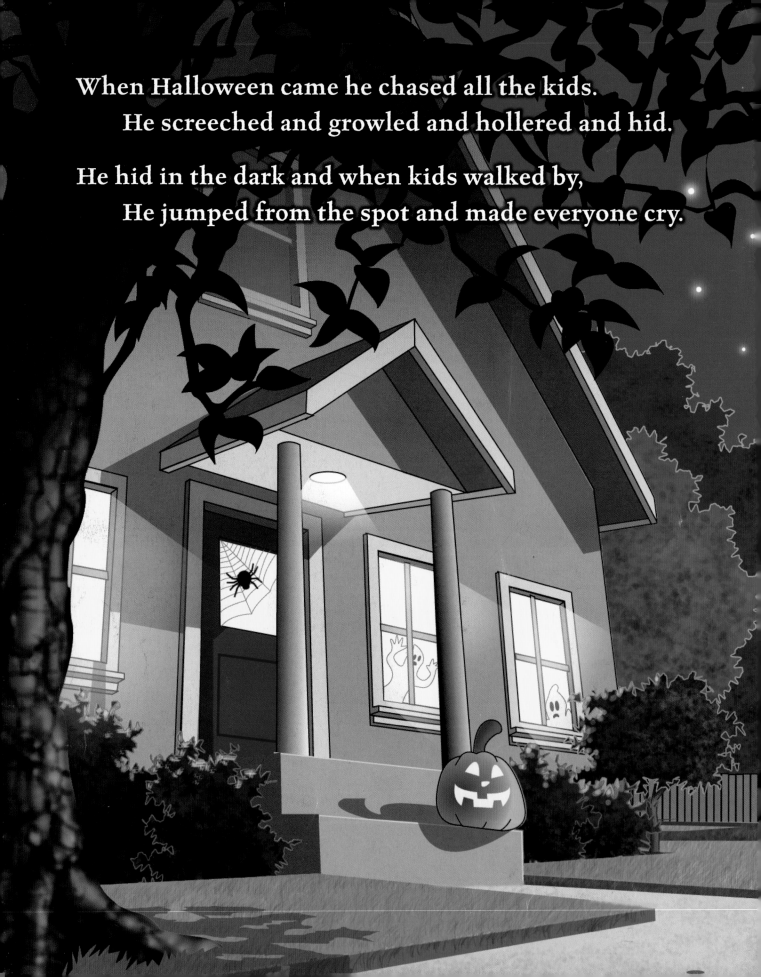

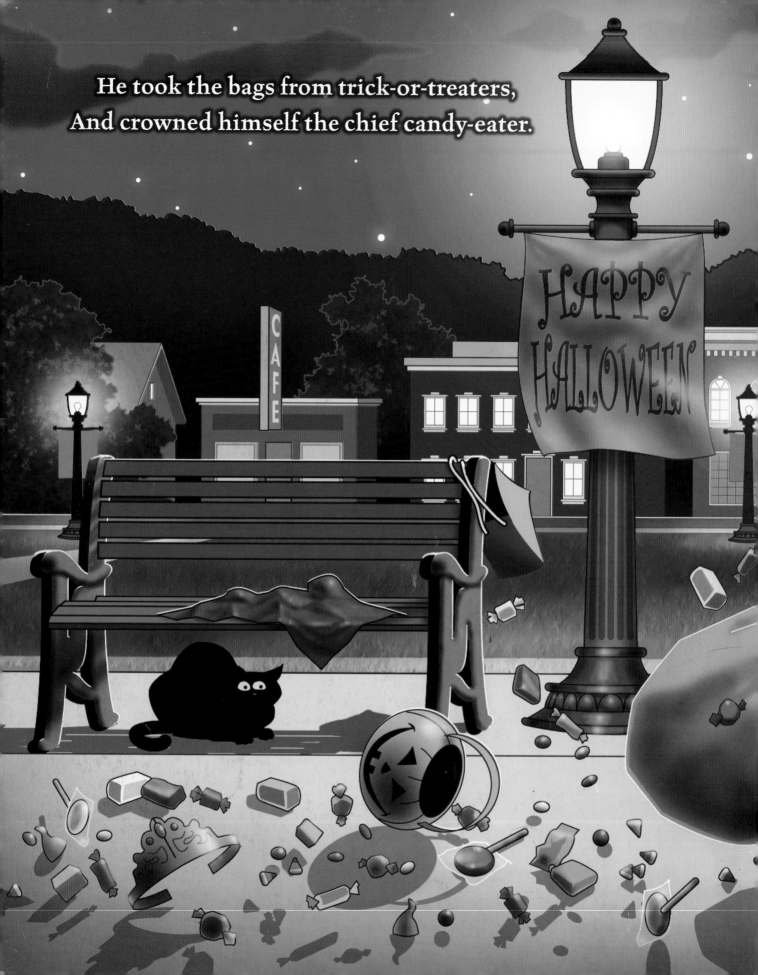

He took the bags from trick-or-treaters,
And crowned himself the chief candy-eater.

He took the kids' candy
and ruined the kids' fun,

And the whole town was
trembling before he was done.

That was his plan, year after year,
    To frighten the people and bring them to tears.

But when he got home to his lonesome old bog,
    There was no one to talk to, except an old frog.

Then one Halloween,
 as he ran through the town,

The Pumpkin Goblin saw one kid
who looked kind of down.

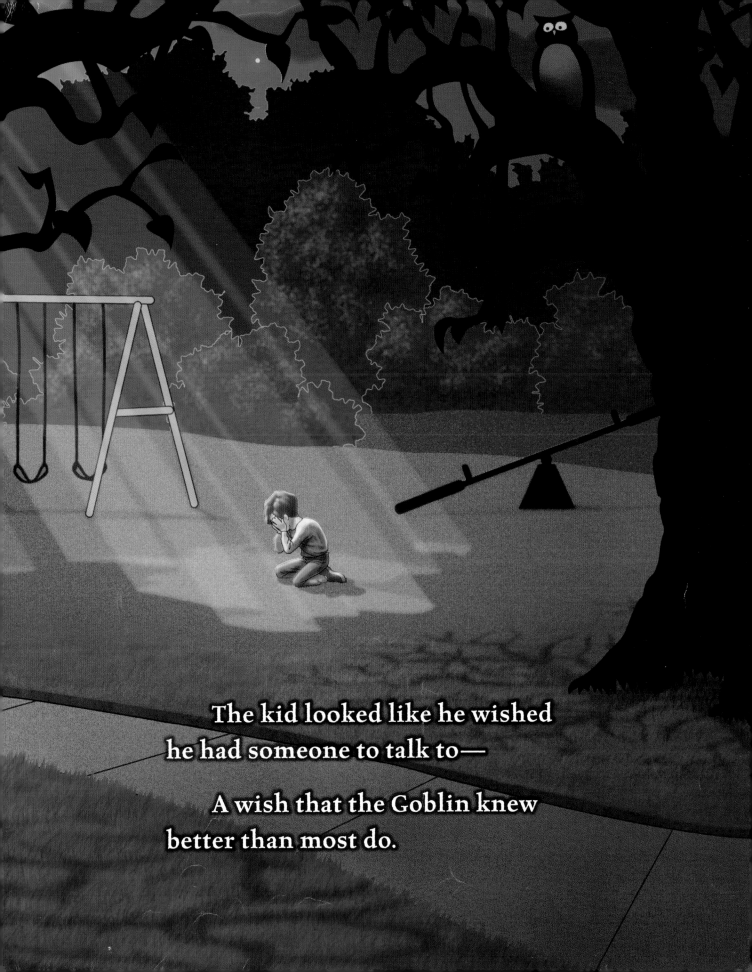

The kid looked like he wished
he had someone to talk to—

A wish that the Goblin knew
better than most do.

From the shadows and dark, the Goblin called out.
He said, "Hello there!" and tried not to shout.

The boy turned around and soon made his choice,
He said "Hi!" to the Goblin with a stuttering voice.

With the town that he'd
frightened for year upon year,

But the town thought of the ways
that he'd filled them with fear...

The Goblin was sleeping,
he'd had quite a night,

But the mob was after him,
searching, all right.

They'd come into the bog
and now they were lost,

And one person only
could help them across

The Pumpkin Goblin stood up and relayed
    That though he'd been scary, they should not be afraid.

He asked for forgiveness, and to be their new friend
    And the town put their Goblin-pie plans to an end.

The Goblin led everyone out of the bog.
   The town didn't eat him (or his pal the old frog).

Brave Fred was the hero, and everyone said,
   There was no point in friends
      if your friends weren't like Fred.

Now on Halloween nights the town trick-or-treaters
Go out with the ex-spooky chief candy-eater.

There's laughter and friendship instead of the screaming,
And it's always in fun that the Goblin is scheming.

So the Pumpkin Goblin
has changed his ways,

And he hangs out with Fred
on most of his days.

But though he might share,
one thing he won't do,

He'll never give up his
Green Muck Worm Stew!

Build Your Own!
Recipe for Green Muck Worm Stew

INGREDIENTS:

Something Green _____

Something Crawly _____

Something Squishy _____

Critters _____

Chunks _____

Other _____

Visit the Pumpkin Goblin to enjoy fun
downloadable activities or to send us
your favorite Green Muck Worm Stew recipe.

www.PumpkinGoblin.com

Author's Note

There have been sightings of Pumpkin Goblins in natural resource areas throughout the world.

This book is dedicated to these wondrous habitats, including the Salmon Creek Watershed in Vancouver, Washington, where the Pumpkin Goblin was originally spotted.